Ms
J

P9-DZA-765

ALL US COME
CROSS THE WATER

All Us Come Cross the Water

HOLT, RINEHART AND WINSTON
New York   Chicago   San Francisco

ISBN: 0-03-089262-7
Library of Congress Catalog Card Number: 72-76575

Printed in the United States of America
Designed by Aileen Friedman

First Edition

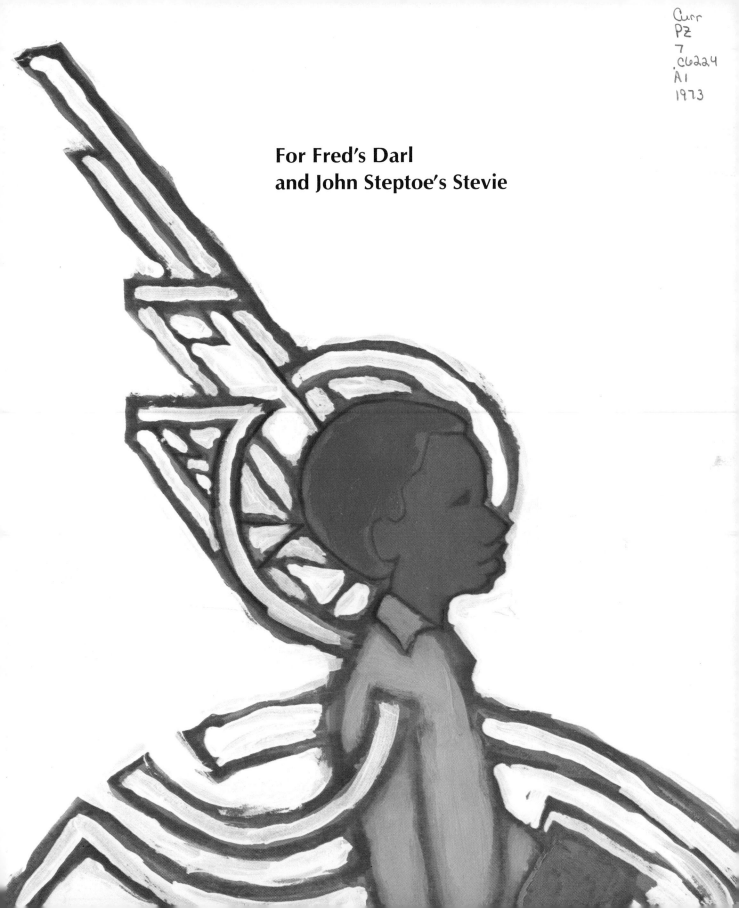

**For Fred's Darl
and John Steptoe's Stevie**

I got this teacher name Miss Wills. This day she come asking everybody to tell where they people come from. Everybody from over in the same place suppose to stand up by theirselves. When it come to me I don't say nothing so she get all mad, cause that make all the other brothers not say nothing too.

"Won't you please cooperate with us, Jim?" she say. I didn't say nothing cause my name is Ujamaa for one thing. So when the bell ring she ask me to stay a little after, so we can talk.

"We must not be ashamed of ourselves, Jim," she say. "You are from a great heritage and you must be proud of that heritage. Now you know you are from Africa, don't you?" she say.

I say, "Yes, mam," and walk on out the place.

First thing, my name is Ujamaa and also Africa is a continent not a country and she say she want everybody to tell what country. Anyhow, I left. The other brothers waiting for me by the light.

Malik say, "That woman is crazy. She get on my nerves."

Bo say, "How come we didn't stan up, Ujamaa? We from Africa!" I just go on home. Bo don't know nothing.

I got a sister name Rose. She studying to be a practical nurse. When she get home I ask her, "Rose where we from?" She come talking about,

"Mama was from Rome, Georgia, and Daddy from Birmingham."

"Before that," I say.

"Mama's Daddy from Georgia too."

"I mean before that too, way back before that." She come laughing talking about,

"They wasn't no way back before that. Before that we was a slave."

I could a punched her in her face. Rose make me sick.

My Daddy's name Nat. He work for the city. When he get home I ask him, "Daddy where we from?"

He say, "What you talking about, boy?"

I say, "I wanna know where did we come from."

He say, "We come up here from Birmingham after your Mama died."

"I mean back before that."

"Boy, I'm too tired to fool with you. Go ask Big Mama them questions."

Big Mama is my Mama's Mama's Mama. She real old and she don't say much, but she see things cause she born with a veil over her face. That make it so she can see spirits and things.

I go up to her and I ask her, "Big Mama, where we come from?"

She say, "Who?"

I say, "Us."

"Which us?"

That's how she talk. She say a lotta stuff you just have to figure out.

I say, "Big Mama, will you tell me where we is all from?" I figure I got her now.

She say, "Why you wanna know?"

I tell her about the teacher and everybody.

She say, "My Mama say her and her Mama was brought from Whydah in Dahomey in 1855." She say, "My Mama was nine years old."

"That mean I'm from Whydah?"

She look at me then.

"Nat's people look like Ashanti people. They come from south in Ghana."

"That mean I'm from Ashanti people?"
She say, "Who are you, boy?"
I say, "I'm Ujamaa."
Shoot, she know who I am, it was her give me my name.
She say, "Go on now then. I'm through."
That's how she is.

I got a grown man friend over to the Panther Book
Shop. Everybody call him Tweezer. We talk about
things sometime and I tell him what I'm gonna be and
all that. He always say, "Just you be a good brother,
Ujamaa." Anyhow, I thought I'd go on over and talk
to him about things and everything. I waited till after
dinner cause we had red beans which I love. Rose
don't like old Tweezer much so when she ask me where
am I going I tell her over to Bo's. She remind me
to be home when the lights go on.

Tweezer sitting out in front of the store, got his wine
in a paper cup. He old but not as old as Big Mama.
People talk about he used to run on the road and
before that he went to college. He real smart. He
know it too always talkin about he a juju man, know
all about magic and stuff like that. He see me coming
down the block and wave.

"Hey, Ujamaa," he kinda grinned.

"Hey, Tweezer," I grinned back.

When I got up to the store he made room for me on
the bench. He didn't say nothing. He never do start
first.

I say, "What's your real name, Tweezer?"
He say, "I don't know."
"How come?"
"It got left."
I say, "Where?"
He say, "In Africa."
"What you mean?"
"When they stole my Daddy's Daddy to
make him a slave they didn't ask for his
name and he didn't give it."
"Well what did they call him?"
He say, "Whatever he let um. Reckon he
figure if they ain't got his name they ain't
really got him."
I say, "Big Mama give me my name. It mean Unity."
He smile then. He start really talking.
"Long as your own give you the name you know it's yours.
We name us. Everybody else just calling us something,
but we name us. You named a good name."

I ask him, "Tweezer, we from all different parts of Africa, how we gonna say what country we from?"

Tweezer say, "We from all them countries, Ujamaa. All off the same boat."

I say, "Some people tell me we wasn't all slaves."

He say, "Wasn't none of us free though. All us crossed the water. We one people, Ujamaa. Boy got that name oughta know that. All us crossed the water."

The lights had to come on just then.

I told Tweezer, "See you later."

"Just be a good brother, brother," Tweezer told me.

Man, I had a whole lot to think about! I'm suppose to lay real still cause I sleep with my Daddy and he got to go to work but Man my mind was going to town. Thing was, what I mostly ended up thinking about was ol Bo and ol Malik and how they didn't even know what was the matter but they went right along with me on the not standing up cause we brothers. And Bo ain't even lived

in this block that long and his Mama is from a island
but we all brothers anyhow. I thought about Tweezer
and him and me being brothers too. All us come cross
the water. Somebody name Ujamaa oughta know that.
I went on to sleep.

Next day everybody in class looking at me
seeing what am I gonna do. Miss Wills got
her mouth all sad think I'm shamed of
something. Pretty soon she say,
"Let us continue yesterday's social studies
lesson, children. We will excuse Jim from the
lesson this time."

Just when she say that I jump up and stand straight as a king, and look right at her and say, "Miss Wills, my name is Ujamaa and that mean Unity and that's where I'm from." Man, Malik and Bo stand right up too, tall as me and just grinning. We all stand there awhile and she don't say nothing. Shoot, she don't even know what we talking about!

ABOUT THE AUTHOR

Lucille Clifton is the author of <u>Some of the Days of Everett Anderson</u> and <u>Everett Anderson's Christmas Coming</u>, picture books of poetry which have been received with great enthusiasm since their publication in 1970 and 1971, respectively. <u>Some of the Days of Everett Anderson</u> was selected for the AIGA Children's Book Show in 1970 and as one of <u>School Library Journal</u>'s Best Books of the Year for 1970. Of <u>Everett Anderson's Christmas Coming</u>, <u>Booklist</u> said it was "universally appealing" and <u>Horn Book</u> wrote, "the verse...sparkles."

Mrs. Clifton's poetry has appeared in <u>Redbook</u>, <u>Highlights for Children</u> and <u>Negro Digest</u>. She feels that her husband, her children and being a Black woman have had the most influence on her writing.

Born in Depew, New York, Mrs. Clifton attended Howard University in Washington, D.C., and now lives in Baltimore, Maryland, with her husband, Fred, and their six young children. When she has free time, she enjoys acting, theater, reading and watching people.

ABOUT THE ARTIST

John Steptoe has in a very short time reached a wide audience of children through his groundbreaking picture books, <u>Stevie</u>, <u>Uptown</u>, <u>Train Ride</u> and <u>Birthday</u>, all of which he both wrote and illustrated. <u>Stevie</u> was chosen as an ALA Notable Children's Book in 1969 and won a Society of Illustrators' Gold Medal in 1970. The John Steptoe Early Childhood Library was opened in Bedford-Stuyvesant, Brooklyn, in November, 1970.

Mr. Steptoe divides his time between New York City, where he grew up, and New England.